Rhyming Inkpen

Pouring Emotions

By

Anupriya Asthana

First Published in 2020

Becomeshakespeare.com
Wordit Content Design & Editing Services Pvt Ltd
Unit - 26, Building A -1, Nr Wadala RTO,
Wadala (East), Mumbai 400037, India
T: +91 8080226699

ISBN - 978-93-89759-45-7

Acknowledgement

First and foremost, I want to thank God. Without his blessings, it won't be possible to publish my first poetry book.

I also want to thank:

My parents and sister,

My best friends,

My social media supporters,

The whole team of BecomeShakespear.com for bringing all my work to you in the form of this book.

Preface

Rhyming Inkpen, Pouring Emotions is a collection of short poems portraying deep feelings of heart and soul. The poems are inspired by the author's life and travel experiences. These short poems are on different aspects of life, love, and nature.

Dedication

This book is dedicated to Ruskin Bond, the author of over
a hundred books of fiction, non-fiction, and poetry.

About the Author

Anupriya Asthana is a solo traveler, photographer, writer, travel blogger and artist who believes in exploring and learning. Professionally she is working as a Technical writer in software. She loves to capture memories and present them to the world in the form of pictures, poems, blogs, and art. She is a winter person and nature lover who doesn't miss a single chance to visit mountains. She believes her soul lives there, close to mother nature.

She is a big fan of Ruskin Bond and her inspiration for writing this book.

Contents

Truth

There is a fine line,

between hope and expectations.

But truth always put

curtain over them!

Unsaid

Some emotions can never be explained,
Some thoughts are always unsaid.

We never find words
suitable to express.

Sometimes they make us happy,
And other times sad.

They will always stay
deep inside our heart!

Heartache

It's an illusion or heartache

which make these weathers.

sometimes blossom & sometimes faded!

Dreams

When we fall in love

with dreams.

Even darkness

shows us light!

Something

Not everything is
for everyone.

But something is
always for everyone.

So rather than chasing
for everything.
Hunt for something!

Soul

Listen to your soul.

No one else can understand
better than us.

All solutions are within us!

Love

Dress me with

the glitter of passion

And I will embrace you with

the warmth of love!

Skin

Take the sheet of maquillage off,
Let your skin reveal the prettiness.

The more glamorous is the soul
than you surmise!

Fantasy

Somewhere in the memory lane,
I found this place.

Exquisite, Noiseless and Utopian
Intimate enough for my sojourn!

Night

Direful was the night,
Edgy was the mind.

The long journey is to conclude,
Give me some sunshine!

Mate

The graciousness you carry,
The softness you have,

Appease my soul
And mend the scars I have!

Words

Propitious were the words,
murmured lovingly.

But wrinkles on the forehead,
cleared all trickery!

Rains

Some may find it shabby,

Some may find it pleasant.

But petrichor has its own revitalizing effect.

Lovers find it lovely,

Brokens find it gloomy.

But it's a season filled with pleasure and jollity!

Freedom of Love

It's not about caste,

Not about religion

And not about gender.

Love is the language of hearts,

To bring souls together!

Writer

When heartaches,
words bleed.

When the mind thinks,
Sleep conceals!

Peace

In the world full of lies,

I found peace in your eyes.

The smile on your face,

Gives the bliss I chase!

Touch

The touch of yours has played,

the strings of my heart.

Soothing it was to surrender my soul,

And rhythmic enough to forget my scars!

Time

Harder was the time,
Passed lonely.

Difficult was the decision,
Taken tactfully!

Moment

Don't know what is wrong what is right,
Let me live this moment a slight.

Don't know how far this will go,
Let me sink in this for more!

Heart

Somehow it is easy

to read mind,

Than to tame

a heart!

Smile

The turbulence
Her heart carry,

Never fades
Her smile's glory!

Pain

Pain poisoned her soul,

In the woodland of dolour.

The warmth of his arms,

Is the only antidote!

Promise

When stars play
Their game,

Even the truest
Promise has to fail!

Alone

O, dear!

Don't underestimate your flair.

Lonely not you are,

Alone you have to shimmer!

New Year

The sheets of memories

you are covering your soul with

Worthless it is

As they cannot bring the extinct.

It's time to perform

With all-new zeal and enthusiasm

So dress yourself in the garment

Woven with experiences & lessons of the past!

The Two

She was tender,

She was warm,

She was the sunshine

in a gloomy hour.

He was cold,

He was naive,

He was a busy bee

focusing on making gain!

Nature

The lush green and mountain high,

The setting sun and dripping sky.

Making me to stay for a while,

To capture memories in my mind.

The earthy smell and foggy dusk,

The fresh breeze and bloomy shrubs.

Telling me to save this heaven,

From greedy eyes and selfish humans!

Warrior

I wish I could stay for a while,

But it's a call of nation's pride.

Mother nation's dignity is in danger,

And my duty is to shelter!

Abode

She was an imaginative decorator,

He was a skilled builder.

How magnificent the abode could have been,

If built together!

Love

Mingled bodies,
Lonely souls.

Broken hearts,
Craving for a cure!

Miss You!

They will propound,
You should move on.

But deep down,
You know it's still not gone!

Perspective

Some find it artistic,

Some find it dramatic.

It's all about perspective,

How we visualize its characteristic!

Nature Song

Hey, wait!

Can you hear that?

A soft rhythmic music.

No, it's not a radio.

No no, it's not even any musical instrument.

Then what can it be?

It's so soulful.

Ah! It's a nature song which mother nature is playing.

Wonderful!

The burbling of the river, the chirping of birds, the
rustling of leaves, the wind sough.

How lovely it is!

Dream

I'm making my own kingdom.

Full of fantasies and freedom

If it's just a hallucination and not real,

Then let me dream and keep this unclear!

Rush

If you make a rush

You will end up into a mess.

So calm your mind

Before something, you have to decide!

Companion

Will, you hold my hand,

To walk down this lane.

Will, you teach me how to stand still,

Even in the toughest state!

Crush

Sipping a cup of coffee

She was flaunting her curls unknowingly.

Sitting in the corner of the eatery,

He was trying to make eye contact knowingly.!

Proposal

Under the sky full of stars,

Wrapping her tight in his arms.

Playing with her tangled curls, slowly he asked,

"Will you be mine?" with a kiss on her palms!

Change

Neither we can cure this alone,

Nor we should play the blame game.

It's a duty of every individual,

Let's do this together to bring a change!

Mother

Mother, not a stage

in the life of a girl.

An emotion it is,

which every girl carries since birth!

Evening of Love

Sitting under the tree,

Waiting for you eagerly.

Lil excitement in my heart,

And full of surprises for you my sweetheart!

Cozy Bed

Home is where I find peace.

After a hectic day, it's my cozy bed that soothes my body and soul.

The soft touch of fabric pampers my every cell,

It makes me forget all the stress.

The satin fabric wraps my skin,

To keep my body warm enough.

The furry pillow cushioned my head,

Like my mother's lap filled with love!

Goodbye

How much destiny

keeps us apart,

You hold a unique place

in my heart!

Memories of Past

I remember the days,

We used to sit for dates.

I still visit this place,

With memories of that phase!

Confront

The moment you accept the truth,

All become lil easy to confront!

Morning Tea

Blend of emotions!

In the form of a potion!

Balance

Good things are felt good,
Because we have faced bad too!

Heights

Crossing odds,

Climbing heights.

The body may wear out,

But this is how the soul revives!

Take a Step

Take a step towards your ambition,

Take a step to follow your passion,

Take a step out of comfort zone,

Towards the gain of your own!

Close

He: How close you are?

She: Close enough to feel your breath,

Close enough to sense your warmth,

Close enough to heal your scars!

Dream or Real

If it's a dream,

Then keep me dreaming.

If it's in real,

Then take me here!

Dress Me

Dress me with jewels of nature,

Simple and sober!

Friends

I will tease you, I will love you,

I will scold you, I will kiss you,

I will beat you, I will hug you,

I will cry with you, I will dance with you,

I will fly with you, I will swim with you,

I will jump with you, I will hike with you,

Because you are my buddy and I can do
anything with you!

Thoughts

Not just me, my tea and breeze,

There were thoughts too,

Accompanying me there.

Dancing in my head,

Taking me somewhere else.

To the land where I'm with you,

Crossing Meadows,

Playing with Lilies,

Holding your hand,

And teasing like silly!

Brother-Sister

Busy life,

Family duties,

Future ambitions,

Chasing dreams.

May take us far from each other

But always remember Dear Sis,

You live in my heart

And I'll stand by you till my last!

Enlighten

Kissing his forehead,

Feeling the intensity.

Slowly she whispered,

Enlighten this naive body!

Life

You are the life
Of my excite,

You are the light
Of my gloomy night!

Valley

Little angels,
Holding hands,
Showering Loveliness,
Guarding this land!

Mountain Breeze

Keep quite,

Yes, you heard it right.

The mountain breeze whispered

To the dancing demons of my mind!

Grey

With passing years their hair turned grey,

But she never missed a single day.

Lighting a lantern on the rooftop,

Looking for his cycle coming down from the hilltop!

Layering

With Deep cuts of

Sorrows, pains and scars.

Layering up with

Smiles, grins and laughs!

Festival

Festive vibes and colourful nights,
Forgetting darkness and accepting lights.

Thanking God and praying for all,
May this festival shower love around the globe!

Little Things

In the race of fulfilling dreams,

Don't forget to enjoy the little things!

Be Kind

Drop the shell

of rudeness,

Reveal the softness

of kindness!

Mixed

I am here

And I am lost.

Floating in dreams,

And sinking in illusions.

Feeling pleasant here

And apprehension inner!

Moon

Among all darkness,
Chaos and loudness,

There is a moon of calmness,
Shining above wickedness
And balancing blackness!

Man

She has night,

She has wine.

Music is on

Grooving with tone.

Earthy smell of lawn,

Mist and fog.

Lighted candles,

Full of Fragrance.

Holding her palm,

He curls her in his arm

Pampering like a child,

He is the man of her life!!

Love Birds

Messy hairs,
Tousled curls.
Wrinkled sheets,
Wrapped curves.

Warm breath,
On his chest.
Deep snores,
In her ears.

Tangled legs,
Truly in love.
Eternal lovebirds,
Under the fur!

Smile

The more you smile,

The more you feel light.

The more you giggle,

The more you spread glitter.

The more you grin,

The more you live!

Into the Wild

No more I scare walking alone,

No more I afraid of getting lost,

No more I ask for the company,

No more I feel lonely!

I have mountains to accompany,

I have trees to shield me,

I have self to protect me,

I have mother nature to look after me!!

Too Young to Be Called Old

Holding a bunch of balloons,

Plucking some wild blooms.

Whistling with blowing wind,

Jumping to catch twigs.

Shouting your name loud,

To heard what mountains back shout.

Would you still call yourself old?

No, Not at all.

You are too young to be called old!

World

Imagine a world

Without Borders in heart,

And immense love

which could not take them apart!!

Special

You have left a special mark on my heart,

Will keep it safe and cherish every hour!

The Moment

It's beautiful to recall,
The moment we had.

It's hard to believe,
It won't come back!

Epilogue

My poetry may have only a few lines,

But they carry deep meaning inside.

The more you will read,

The more you will feel,

How connecting are the words

With your life and dreams.

With Love,

Anupriya Asthana